Felicity Wishes

Storytelling Stars

and other stories

Hodder
Children's
Books

A division of Hachette Children's Books

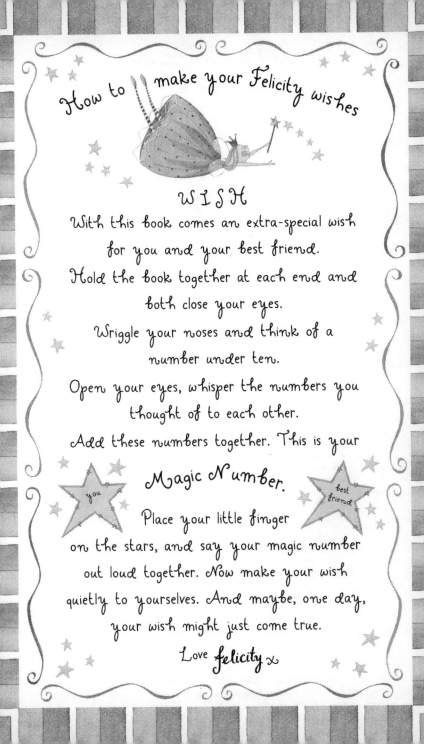

How to make your Felicity wishes

WISH

With this book comes an extra-special wish
for you and your best friend.

Hold the book together at each end and
both close your eyes.

Wriggle your noses and think of a
number under ten.

Open your eyes, whisper the numbers you
thought of to each other.

Add these numbers together. This is your

Magic Number.

you

best friend

Place your little finger
on the stars, and say your magic number
out loud together. Now make your wish
quietly to yourselves. And maybe, one day,
your wish might just come true.

Love felicity x

For Louise and Heather,
with thanks. x

FELICITY WISHES
Felicity Wishes © 2000 Emma Thomson
Licensed by White Lion Publishing

Text and Illustrations © 2007 Emma Thomson

First published in Great Britain in 2007 by Hodder Children's Books

The right of Emma Thomson to be identified as the author and illustrator of this work has
been asserted by her in accordance with the Copyright, Designs and Patents Act 1988.

I

A Catalogue record for this book is available from the British Library.

ISBN: 9 780 34094395 3

Printed in the UuK by CPI Bookmarque, Croydon, CRO 4TD

The paper and board used in this paperback by Hodder Children's Books are natural recyclable
products made from wood grown in sustainable forests. The manufacturing processes
conform to the environmental regulations of the country of origin.

Hodder Children's Books
A division of Hachette Children's Books, 338 Euston Road, London NWI 3BH
An Hachette Livre UuK Company

CONTENTS

The Adventures of Shirley Helmes

Book Bamboozle

Felicity Wishes was in her English class at school – but she wasn't paying attention!

"Felicity, what topic have you chosen?" asked Miss Pen.

Felicity looked up sheepishly at the teacher.

"I haven't chosen one. I don't know what to do," she replied quietly. "I looked in the library like you said, but I couldn't find anything."

Miss Pen had set the class individual

projects, writing about subjects of their choice. It was easy for Holly, Polly, Daisy and Winnie. Holly loved anything to do with fashion and had decided to write about the development of fashion through the ages. Polly wanted to find out more about being a Tooth Fairy. Daisy chose to write about plants and flowers and their natural habitats, and Winnie was doing her project on the great fairy adventurers of the past. They had all tried to help Felicity, but none of them could think of a topic that interested her.

"Don't worry, come and see me after class, Felicity," Miss Pen said kindly, with a reassuring smile.

"We'll see you by the Large Oak Tree," Polly called when the lesson was over. She fluttered out of the classroom and into the warm sunshine outside, while Felicity stayed behind.

"Right then, Felicity," Miss Pen began.

"Can't you think of anything to write your project on?"

Felicity shook her head.

"And you couldn't find anything in the library?" Miss Pen continued.

"No, nothing," Felicity replied.

"Well, there's one other place you could try."

Just then there was a knock at the door and Miss Fossil, the history teacher, fluttered in. She swooped up to Miss Pen's desk, put down a note and quickly turned to fly back out of the classroom – without uttering a single word.

Meanwhile Miss Pen continued to talk to Felicity, without any sign that she'd seen Miss Fossil.

"As I was saying, have you ever been to Little Blossoming Bookshop?" Miss Pen asked.

Felicity shook her head. She'd never even heard of it.

"It has old and new books on every topic imaginable. It's always worth a try if there's nothing in the library," Miss Pen told her. Then she drew Felicity a map of where to go and Felicity left to join her friends.

* * *

"It was very strange! She didn't say a word," said Felicity, now sitting under the Large Oak Tree.

She had just told Holly, Polly, Winnie and Daisy about Miss Fossil coming in to see Miss Pen and neither fairy speaking to the other.

"Actually, I'm not sure I've ever seen

them talking," said Polly thoughtfully.

For the rest of the day the fairies carefully watched Miss Fossil and Miss Pen. They sat at opposite ends of the teachers' table in the cafeteria

at lunchtime, they didn't look at each other when they passed in the corridor, they were never both in the staffroom at the same time, and they left the school by different doors at the end of the day.

"It's very odd," said Daisy as the fairies fluttered home. "The other teachers talk to each other all the time. I wonder what they fell out about."

Felicity was wondering exactly the same thing as she left her friends to go and find the bookshop. She arranged to meet them in Sparkles, the café on the corner, after she had finished.

* * *

"It can't be down here," she thought to herself as she came to a very narrow street with old houses along each side. The houses seemed to lean into the cobbled road, blocking out the sunlight. Felicity checked her map for the tenth time. It was definitely the right place, so Felicity took a deep breath and carried on. She was almost at the end of the street when she caught a glimpse of something on her right.

"Oh!" she exclaimed.

Tucked away between two houses

was Little Blossoming Bookshop, with big arched windows and a double door at the front. As Felicity turned the handle to enter, bells jingled and a small fairy with a ponytail looked up from behind the counter to say "hello".

"Can I help you?" the fairy asked, smiling.

"No, thank you, I'm just looking," Felicity replied, amazed at the amount of books crammed into the shop.

The shelves all looked very old.

They were wooden along one side and marble along the other.

The fairy with the ponytail saw Felicity looking around.

"It used to be a general store," she informed Felicity. "All the cold food like butter and cheese was kept on the marble, and all the dried food on the wooden shelves. And the flour and tea were kept in those," she said, pointing to large metal tins under the shelves with big numbers painted on them. "We can't change a thing in here, it has to stay just as it is!"

Felicity smiled. Everything did look very old, including the comfy armchair in one corner and the old suitcases stacked with books. Felicity didn't know where to start. There was a section of books on cookery, one on gardening, several shelves on sport, travel, biographies of famous fairies and every other topic imaginable!

Then she glanced to her right and saw a glass-fronted cabinet with very old books inside.

"What are these?" she asked the assistant.

"Some of them are first editions, some are out of print and very rare, others are just very old," the assistant said, fluttering over to stand with Felicity. She took out a key and opened the cabinet. "Feel free to have a look, but please handle the books with care."

Felicity looked along the shelves at the old books until she came to one that looked very interesting.

"Friendship: The History of Fairy Interaction and Etiquette," she read aloud.

The assistant had gone to help another fairy so Felicity very carefully took the book off the shelf and fluttered to one of the armchairs to sit down and have a look.

The book creaked as Felicity opened it, as though it hadn't been touched for years.

As Felicity turned the pages something fell out of the book and into her lap. It was a letter, addressed to "Lottie, Valley View, Flying Downs, Little Blossoming". As Felicity turned it over, she saw that it hadn't been opened.

It all seemed very mysterious to Felicity: the yellowing paper, the curly, old-fashioned handwriting, the old book. Perhaps Lottie had never got the letter and didn't know what was inside. It could be very important, something life-changing even. Felicity decided that the only thing to do was open the letter, just in case she could find out anything about Lottie and deliver it to her.

Felicity didn't have any idea what the letter was about but it sounded important. What if Lottie had never read the letter?

Dear Lottie,

I've decided to give you this book to show you how sorry I am. We cannot both be Friendship Fairies so I think that you should be and I will find something else I am good at. I should never have reacted in the way I did and I am truly sorry. I hope you will forgive me. Wanting to do the same thing just shows how similar we are.

Your friend for ever,
Cherry

Felicity quickly copied it down into her notebook, put the book back in the cabinet and rushed out of the shop to go and find her friends.

* * *

"What if they never made friends and they're still arguing now?" said Daisy as Felicity told her friends about the letter.

"Exactly," Felicity replied. "That's why I'm going to find Lottie and Cherry and make sure they sorted out their differences."

"How are you going to do that?" Holly asked, amazed at Felicity's determination.

"I'm not sure," Felicity said thoughtfully. "But I'll think of something!"

* * *

After school the next day Felicity went straight back to the bookshop.

"Hello again!" the cheery assistant said as Felicity entered. "How can I help you today?"

"Well, I was wondering," Felicity replied, leading the fairy back to the cabinet and taking the book out, "where this book came from."

The assistant frowned. "I don't know. It's been here longer than I have. Let me check our records and see if I can find out for you."

The assistant fluttered away and Felicity settled down to have another look at the book.

"Aha!" the assistant said a few minutes later. Felicity flew over to the counter.

"It says here the book was donated by a novice fairy studying at the School of Nine Wishes," she said, pointing to a very large book on the counter in front of her. "It looks like she'd given up her dream of being a Friendship Fairy. That's the only reason she would give the book away."

Felicity thanked the assistant for her help and left to find her friends.

"Perhaps Lottie gave the book away without knowing the letter was inside," Polly said when Felicity had finished telling them the latest news.

"I've got to find out who Lottie is and give her the letter," said Felicity. "I just don't know how."

"Can't you just go to the address on the envelope?" Daisy asked.

Felicity smiled. "Why didn't I think of that! Thanks, Daisy. OK, who's coming?" Felicity jumped up and looked at her friends. None of them had moved.

"What are you going to say?" Polly asked. "You won't know if it's the right fairy and, even if it is, it was all in the past. She's probably forgotten all about it."

Felicity slumped back down in her chair.

"You're right," she said sadly. "But I have to do something."

"You could knock on the neighbours' doors and say you're an old friend looking for Lottie!" Winnie suggested. "You'll have to be very inconspicuous though! You need to make sure they don't know who you are."

Felicity giggled. "Shall I wear a disguise? Like a raincoat, sunglasses and a hat?"

"No, silly. Everyone would think you're even more suspicious then! You need to act like you're very scatty and you've forgotten Lottie's address," Polly continued, agreeing with Winnie.

"He-he! That shouldn't be hard!" Felicity chuckled.

"Then ask breezily if anyone knows where she lives. We'll all come and help you," Holly finished.

Felicity did just as her friends said, starting at the end of the road. Holly, Polly, Winnie and Daisy all hid behind fences and trees, hedges and lamp-posts as Felicity knocked on doors and spoke to the fairies inside as casually as she could.

By the fifth house she got to, only two doors away from Valley View, the house on the envelope, the fairy inside knew Lottie.

"Yes, she lives just there!" the fairy said, pointing to Valley View. "Of course, not many fairies know her as Lottie. We usually call her Miss Pen."

Felicity nearly fell over in shock.

"Miss Pen?" she asked uncertainly.

"Yes, she teaches English at the

School of Nine Wishes. Surely you know that?" the fairy answered.

Felicity nodded and smiled, then thanked the fairy for her help and went to join her friends.

"It's Miss Pen," she told them, still in shock.

"Oh, where?" Polly said, looking around her. "I need to talk to her about my latest homework project."

"No, it's Miss Pen! Lottie is Miss Pen!" Felicity explained. "All along she's been right here! She told me about the bookshop and she gave them the book all those years ago!"

"But we still don't know who gave Miss Pen the book," said Holly. "Who is Cherry?"

"And who would ever fall out with Miss Pen?" mused Daisy. "She's friends with everyone."

Suddenly, it all fell into place for Felicity. "What if it's Miss Fossil?" she squealed. "What if Miss Fossil is Cherry and she wrote the letter, but Miss Pen never found it and that's why they're still not talking!"

"That's it!" Polly said, hugging her clever friend. "All we have to do now is make sure Miss Fossil's name is Cherry, then the mystery is solved!"

Polly clapped her hands.

"Not quite. They're still not talking," Holly pointed out.

But Felicity knew that wouldn't be a problem. She already had an idea.

* * *

The next day at school Felicity asked Miss Meandering, the geography teacher, what Miss Fossil's first name was and discovered that it was indeed

Cherry. Then during her lunch break she flew as fast as she could to the bookshop and, after explaining the situation, asked if she could borrow the book on friendship, promising to look after it and return it safely that night.

Back at school, she sneaked into Miss Pen's classroom while it was empty and placed the book on her desk, the letter open on top.

Then Felicity and her friends silently waited in the corridor for Miss Pen to return from her lunch. When she did it was only a matter of seconds before she came flying back out of her room and passed the fairies so quickly that she didn't even see they were there.

The fairies silently followed her all the way to Miss Fossil's classroom. Miss Pen burst in, the letter in her hand, apologizing to Miss Fossil.

"I gave the book away without ever

seeing the letter. I didn't know you'd given up on your dream too. I thought you didn't like me any more," Miss Pen gushed to a very confused-looking Miss Fossil.

"Slow down, Lottie. Whatever do you mean?" Miss Fossil asked her old friend.

"I just found the book on my desk with the letter inside. I never read the letter all those years ago."

As Miss Pen explained her discovery to Miss Fossil and Miss Fossil slowly began to understand, there was only one mystery left to solve.

"So who put the book on your desk?" Miss Fossil asked.

Felicity smiled from the corridor outside where she was listening, and thought she would leave them to work out the mystery for themselves. The two teachers were happy again – and Felicity had something to write her project about: the importance of friendship.

A true friendship will survive

the good times
and the bad

Storytelling Stars

Since discovering a bookshop in Little Blossoming, Felicity Wishes hadn't stopped reading. She always seemed to have her head in a book, wherever she went.

"Felicity, can't you put it down, just for a minute?" Polly asked, tapping Felicity on the shoulder to get her attention as they sat under the Large Oak Tree one lunchtime.

"Hang on, it's a really good bit," Felicity replied from behind the book as she turned the page.

Felicity had never before read so many books and her friends just couldn't understand where her new enthusiasm had come from.

The truth was that since Felicity had found Little Blossoming Bookshop, the assistants there had introduced her to many different kinds of books. Some were books she'd never even thought of reading before – and she simply couldn't finish one quickly enough to start another!

"I've got a pile of books next to my bed taller than me!" she told her friends. "I'm going to have to give up sleeping just to read them all!"

Felicity loved having so many books to read. Her friends Holly, Polly, Winnie and Daisy all had their own interests, and although Felicity enjoyed cooking and dancing she found that she enjoyed reading even more.

* * *

"Good morning, Felicity!" called Heather, the friendly assistant, as Felicity went into the bookshop one sunny Saturday morning. "I was hoping you would come in today. I've got something for you!"

Heather held up a glittering poster as Felicity went to have a closer look.

BEGIN A BOOK CLUB TODAY!

If you have a passion for reading, why not start a book club with your friends. All you need is lots of books and somewhere to meet. Enjoy!

Felicity thought it sounded very exciting and, after thanking Heather for thinking of her, rushed out of the bookshop and immediately called her friends for an emergency meeting.

"What's the rush?" panted Holly as she fluttered into Sparkles, the café on the corner. "I got here as quickly as I could."

Daisy was immediately behind her. "What's wrong, Felicity?" she puffed, looking concerned.

Felicity waited for Polly and Winnie, who arrived seconds later equally out of breath, and spoke to her friends all at once.

"I popped into the bookshop this morning," Felicity began, while all her friends rolled their eyes, "and Heather gave me this!" She brandished the poster triumphantly as her friends leant in closer.

"A book club?" Holly said, wrinkling

her nose. "Why would we want to join a book club?"

"I thought it would be a good idea," Felicity said, disappointed Holly didn't feel the same.

"Would we have to read lots of boring books?" Daisy asked gently.

"No, we'd be able to pick whichever books we wanted to read," Felicity answered.

"So how would it work?" Winnie asked, intrigued.

Felicity explained that each fairy had to choose a book they wanted everyone to read. Then they would all go away and read the book – and get together a week later to talk about it.

"It's an excellent idea, Felicity!" said Polly, smiling. Polly loved books just as much as Felicity.

"So we could all read a book on fashion?" Holly asked.

"Whatever you choose!" Felicity replied.

Holly seemed much happier. "Stella Fluttiano has just written her first-ever novel, all about a fairy fashion icon who disappears from a fashion show only to reappear ten years later in the same place. I've been dying to read it!"

"Let's start with that then!" Felicity beamed. "Everyone needs to get a copy and read it by next week. We'll meet next Saturday at my house!"

The fairies all agreed and went off to find the book straight away.

* * *

A week later, Holly, Polly, Winnie and Daisy arrived at Felicity's house to find a colourful poster on her front door.

Felicity opened the door with a huge smile on her face.

"Welcome, welcome!" she sang. "Please take a seat," she said, ushering them into her sitting room. None of the fairies could believe their eyes!

Set out on Felicity's coffee table was the largest selection of nibbles and drinks they had ever seen.

"I've been doing a bit of cooking! So far I've not burnt anything!" Felicity said, just as the smoke alarm began to beep in her kitchen.

"Oops!" she called, rushing out of the room.

She came back with a tray of what looked like tiny sugar books, slightly black around the edges.

"They're still beautiful!" said Daisy, appreciating all the effort Felicity had gone to set up their first meeting.

Once the fairies were all seated they began to discuss the book. They talked for so long that when they glanced out of the window they were surprised to see it was already dark!

Daisy told them about a new book she wanted to read and said the next meeting could be at her house.

That night Felicity was very happy. Perhaps some of her new-found enthusiasm for books was rubbing off on her friends!

* * *

The next week the fairies met again and discussed Daisy's book. It was all about a secret greenhouse filled with the most magical plants in Fairy World, and two fairies who discovered it in an overgrown garden.

"It inspired me!" Winnie said, leading the discussion. "I've never really noticed plants before but now, wherever I travel, they will be the first thing I look at!"

Once again the fairies chatted well into the night.

"Who wants to choose the next book?" asked Felicity as the fairies were getting ready to leave.

"I will!" cried Polly, before the others even had a chance to open their mouths. "It can be at my house. A brand-new book has just been published fictionalizing the life of Carlotta Bronty, a famous novelist from the past."

* * *

For the next two weeks the fairies read

Polly's book, discussed it at her house, and then they read Winnie's book. Finally, it was time for Felicity to choose the book she wanted them all to read.

"At last!" Felicity exclaimed. "It feels like I've been waiting for ever! And I've got a great book for us all to read!"

"What is it, Felicity?" Daisy asked excitedly.

"It's called…" Felicity paused dramatically, "*Woodland Diary*."

Daisy squealed with delight. "Is it all about trees and plants found in woodlands?" she asked.

"Not quite," Felicity replied. "It's about five fairies who go into a wood and completely disappear. All that is found is their diary."

"It might mention the plants they see in the wood," said Daisy hopefully.

"It's a very old book," Felicity explained. "I found it right at the back of the bookshop, hidden from view on a top shelf. The thing is, there was only one copy so I think we'll have to share."

"Well, why don't we have a sleepover tomorrow night?" Polly suggested. "The sooner we start, the more chance we've got of finishing it before next weekend."

"Excellent idea! My house tomorrow then!" Felicity said. "I'll prepare some nibbles!"

* * *

"I searched on my computer and found some information about the book!" Felicity told her friends when they arrived the next day. "Apparently it's a true story."

"Really?" Holly asked.

"Really," Felicity affirmed. "I found a newspaper article from when it was published. It said that the original diary

41

had just been found, covered over with leaves, in a forest. Six months earlier, five fairies had gone camping for half-term and had never been seen again. They were just novice fairies like us, and no one knew they were missing until they didn't turn up for school when half-term was over."

Daisy's wings quivered. "It sounds a bit scary to me," she said.

"It sounds like an adventure to me!" said Winnie excitedly.

The fairies all squeezed on to Felicity's sofa and Felicity, right in the middle, started reading.

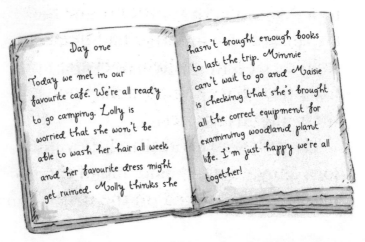

Day one

Today we met in our favourite café. We're all ready to go camping. Lolly is worried that she won't be able to wash her hair all week and her favourite dress might get ruined. Molly thinks she hasn't brought enough books to last the trip. Minnie can't wait to go and Maisie is checking that she's brought all the correct equipment for examining woodland plant life. I'm just happy we're all together!

Felicity kept reading for over an hour, until her throat was very dry. Then they took it in turns. As it started to get dark outside strange things started to happen in the book. First, Maisie lost her bag. She had only put it down for a second to look at a flower, but it had gone when she went to pick it up.

"Poor Maisie," said Holly, who had been reading. "All her clothes, just gone!"

"I'm sure her friends shared theirs with her," said Daisy.

But one by one all the other fairies lost their bags too, until no one had anything but what they had been holding or had in their pockets: Christie's diary, Minnie's map and their mobile phones.

Then the fairies realized they were lost. They couldn't find any of the nature trails marked on the map and

hadn't passed a picnic site for hours.
As it started to get dark in the wood,
they realized their torches had been
in their bags, so they weren't able to
see where they were going.

"I don't like this very much," Daisy

said, squeezing closer to Polly who was sitting next to her.

As the night drew in, the fairies' Woodland Diary entry recorded that they'd decided to call for help but their phones didn't have a signal. They tried to find a way home but couldn't find any way out of the wood – the more they walked, the deeper they went. Then it got windy and the strange noises started.

By this time it wasn't only Daisy who was scared. Felicity, Holly, Polly and Winnie had all squeezed in closer to each other, leaving large gaps at either end of the sofa.

"Do we have to keep reading?" Holly asked.

"We have to find out what happens. It's bound to be all right in the end. Most stories have a happy ending," Winnie said, taking the book to read for a while.

But the book just got scarier and scarier. By the end the fairies were shaking uncontrollably.

"But what happens next? Where did the fairies go?" Polly asked, her teeth chattering.

"That's it!" said Winnie, closing the book and setting it carefully down on Felicity's coffee table. "There is no more. The Woodland Diary entry ends abruptly on day thirteen."

None of the fairies said anything for a long time. Eventually, Holly broke the silence.

"Are your doors and windows locked, Felicity?" she asked.

Felicity jumped up to make sure.

"I don't think I'll ever visit a wood at night again," Daisy said, her voice trembling.

The fairies turned on all the lights in the house, then crept up to Felicity's room. They checked carefully under

Felicity's bed, in every cupboard and
behind every door before they climbed
into the bed, pulling the covers up to
their eyes. But it was no use. None of
the fairies could sleep.

They spent a very long night whispering to each other and hugging their teddies tightly, until at last the sun began to rise over the hills.

"Finally," Felicity said, yawning. "I can't wait to get to school!"

* * *

It took the fairies half an hour longer than usual to get to school, because none of them wanted to fly over Nine Wish Wood. But they still arrived early.

"Whatever is the matter, girls?" Fairy Godmother asked, as soon as she saw them in the playground. Each of the fairies was still shaking from the tips of her wings to the ends of her toes, and they were all a ghostly shade of white, with dark rings under their eyes from lack of sleep.

"Nothing, Fairy Godmother," Polly replied squeakily. "We just stayed up a little later than usual."

"Well, you should all get an early

night tonight," Fairy Godmother said,
fluttering away.

Each fairy shuddered at the thought of ever spending the night alone again.

"Can we stay at your house again tonight?" Holly asked Felicity.

"Please!" Felicity replied desperately.

* * *

The first lesson of the day was English and as the fairies settled into their seats, Felicity, Holly, Polly, Winnie and Daisy all pushed their chairs closer towards one another. Miss Pen entered the classroom.

"Felicity, Holly, Polly, Winnie and Daisy, there is plenty of space in this classroom and no need to sit on top of each other! Spread your chairs out, fairies!"

The friends reluctantly did as they were told and could hardly concentrate throughout the lesson.

At the very end Miss Pen gave them their homework.

"This term I have found you a very

interesting book to read. There was a lot of controversy surrounding its launch a long, long time ago."

Miss Pen opened the drawer in her desk and pulled out a book.

Daisy gasped loudly, Holly turned almost translucent and Felicity fell off her chair with shock!

Miss Pen tutted at the fairies' strange behaviour and continued.

"*Woodland Diary*. I doubt any of you will have heard of this book – it is rather old. At the time of its release, it was marketed as a true story, and several newspaper articles claimed it as such. But I am happy to tell you that it is only fiction!"

Polly's eyes widened in disbelief. "It's not a real diary after all?" she squealed.

"The camping trip was all made up?" burst out Holly.

"Yes," Miss Pen replied, confused.

"Don't tell me you fairies have heard of it?" she asked.

Felicity started giggling and heaved a huge sigh of relief.

"You could say that!" she said, smiling at her friends. They all started to giggle along with her.

friends can help you smile

even through the
scariest moments

Bookworm Baffle

It hadn't stopped raining in Little
Blossoming for days and Felicity
Wishes was very bored. All her friends
were busy – Daisy was looking after
the flowers she had just planted in
her greenhouse, Winnie was planning
her next adventure, Polly was helping
out at the Tooth Fairy Agency, and
Holly was making lots of new clothes.
Felicity just didn't know what to do.

Then suddenly she had an idea!

"I know, I'll go back to the bookshop. Maybe I'll find a brilliant book to lose myself in!" she thought.

A few weeks ago, Felicity had visited Little Blossoming Bookshop for the very first time. She'd loved the bookshop, with its comfy armchairs, old fittings and warm and cosy atmosphere.

Grabbing her raincoat and umbrella, Felicity flew over to the bookshop.

"Good morning!" the fairy behind the counter called as Felicity entered. "Can I help you?"

"Yes, I hope so," Felicity replied. "I'm looking for something exciting!"

"Every book is exciting to me!" the fairy chuckled.

"I don't want anything too difficult. I want something I can lose myself in. A good story, but not too long, and something I haven't read before!"

Felicity said, unsure that any such book existed.

"Hmmmm, let me see," said the assistant as Felicity followed her over to the old books in the back corner of the shop.

"Aha!" she said, taking a book out. "Have you ever read *The Adventures of Shirley Helmes*?"

Felicity shook her head. She'd never even heard of it!

"Excellent!" the assistant grinned, handing Felicity the book. "You'll love it! This is a first edition, so it must stay in the bookshop at all times, but feel free to have a gentle look through. Why don't you read a few pages and, if you like it, I can order you a new copy. It will arrive in a few days."

Felicity thanked the fairy and sat down in one of the comfy armchairs, where the assistant brought her a cup of complimentary hot chocolate!

Felicity read the first few pages of the book and started to enjoy it straight away. Shirley Helmes, the main character, was a detective fairy who had been asked to solve the mystery of the missing statues. Statues were going missing from different towns in Fairy World and reappeared weeks later in different places, mysteriously cleaned and mended. The first statue that went missing was a giant bird. Once upon a time it had been bright blue, but had faded to grey over time and its beak had been broken for years. Then all of a sudden it went missing – only to reappear, miles away, and as good as new!

Felicity was so absorbed in the book that she hadn't noticed another fairy enter the shop. It was only when Felicity realized her hot chocolate had gone cold that she looked up.

"Oh, hello!" she said to the fairy

hovering in front of her. Felicity
noticed that she was wearing an odd
purple hat with a flower sticking out
of it.

"That book looks old," the fairy said
bluntly. "Are the pages falling out?"

Felicity looked back down at the
book. "No, I don't think so," she replied
uncertainly, looking through it carefully.
"Should they be?"

"No, I was just wondering," the fairy

said, before she swished away to the
other side of the shop.

Felicity looked up at the large clock
on the back wall of the shop and
jumped when she realized it was a
quarter to three already. She was meant
to meet Holly, Polly, Daisy and Winnie
in Sparkles, the café on the corner, at
two!

"Don't worry, that clock's wrong.
It always says quarter to three!" the
assistant said, noticing Felicity
scrambling out of her chair. "It's
actually only twenty to two!"

Felicity sighed. "Oh, thank you!" she
said, fluttering over to the assistant. "I
didn't realize the time, I was so lost in
the book. It's excellent!"

The assistant smiled. "Would you like
me to order you a copy?"

"Well, erm, yes, but," Felicity stuttered,
"I'm not sure I can wait a few days to
read the rest!"

"You're welcome to come back any time and read that copy," the assistant said kindly.

Felicity reluctantly left the book with the assistant and went to find her friends, eager to return to the bookshop as soon as possible.

* * *

"They're just starting to come through the soil!" Daisy was saying excitedly as Felicity entered Sparkles. "I was up talking to them all night. I can't wait to get back!"

Felicity ordered a milkshake and sat down in the armchair by the fire as Polly stifled a huge yawn.

"Long night, Poll?" Felicity asked her friend.

"I've never been out collecting teeth so late!" Polly replied. "The sweetshop has just introduced a new sticky toffee humbug and it seems that every fairy in Little Blossoming with a wobbly

tooth tried it! We collected a record
number of teeth last night!"

Winnie was busily flicking through
holiday brochures.

"I just can't decide where to go!"
she said, exasperated, pointing at the
pictures. "I've been there and there
and there. I can't go there until I
qualify as an Adventure Fairy, so that
only leaves there and there."

Felicity leant over to look at the
brochure, but she hadn't been to any
of the places Winnie was deliberating
over so she couldn't really help.

"How are the dresses coming along, Holly?" she asked.

"Almost finished!" Holly replied. "I've just got to sew the skirts on to the tops and I'm all done! I could have finished if I'd just had a bit more time."

Felicity loved spending time with her friends, but it seemed they all had other things they wanted to get back to. And she couldn't wait to see what happened in the rest of the book! So Felicity and her friends arranged to meet again in a couple of days and they all flew off in their different directions.

* * *

When Felicity went back into the bookshop, both the assistant fairies were standing behind the counter, deep in conversation.

"I just can't understand it!" said one with short, spiky hair who Felicity hadn't seen before. "Three books in one morning. It's outrageous!"

The fairy who had helped Felicity that morning agreed. "We'll have no books left before long!"

She smiled when she saw Felicity.

"Is everything OK?" Felicity asked, concerned.

"Our books keep going missing!" the fairy with short hair replied. "Just disappearing off the shelf! It's a mystery! And it's not just us; it's happening in the bookshops in Bloomfield too and all the libraries in the area."

The other assistant smiled and handed Felicity *The Adventures of Shirley Helmes*. "Your book is still here, though. Enjoy!"

As Felicity settled back down to read, she couldn't stop thinking about the odd fairy who had spoken to her that morning.

"But we've had hardly any customers!" the assistant with short hair was saying. "It just doesn't make sense."

Felicity cleared her throat and got back up to talk to the fairies.

"Actually, I did see one other fairy in here this morning," Felicity began.

"She was wearing a funny purple hat with a flower sticking out the side, and she asked me if my book was falling apart."

"Oh, that's Jerry!" the assistant said, smiling. "She's in here all the time. She's not the kind of fairy to take books."

Felicity went back to her detective story, wondering about the missing books.

Shirley Helmes had just discovered a pattern to the missing statues and had worked out which ones might go missing next. She had decided to position herself by one of the statues and wait for something to happen.

That was it! Felicity realized, jumping out of her chair.

"Which books have gone missing so far?" she asked the assistants, her wings quivering with excitement.

The fairies busily tapped away at

their computer and printed out a list.

"They're all from the collection of old books we keep. I don't know why anyone would want to take them – they're mostly tatty and falling apart."

Felicity took the list and went to the shelf. So far the authors' surnames had begun with the letters A, B, C, D or E – so that must mean F was next! Felicity fluttered around the F shelf and pulled out three books that were particularly tatty or damaged. She jotted down their titles and authors and put them back exactly where she had found them.

"I've had an idea!" Felicity said to the assistants, and quickly explained her plan.

* * *

The next day, Felicity went to the bookshop early, getting soaked in the rain on her way.

"Good morning!" she said to the assistants as she entered. "Have any more books gone missing?"

"Yes! Three already!" The fairy with short hair replied. The day before, she had introduced herself as Heather. She gave Felicity a list of the books – and they were the exact ones that Felicity had written down the day before!

"Hmmmm," Felicity said, tapping her chin with her finger as she thought about what to do next. "Have you had many customers today?"

"Only a few," Heather replied. "I'll ask Louisa if she had many customers before I got here."

A few minutes later, Heather came out of the office at the back of the bookshop, followed by another fairy with short red hair.

"I haven't been here for a few days," she told Felicity. "I understand more books have gone missing. Can you help?"

"I think I can. Have you noticed any customers acting strangely this morning?" Felicity asked.

"Well, Jerry came in as usual and a few other fairies. No one out of the ordinary, though," Louisa replied.

"Hmmm," Felicity said, tapping her chin again.

She settled back into the armchair, this time keeping one eye on her book and the other on the old books section, particularly the bookshelf with authors beginning with the letter G.

Few fairies came into the bookshop all afternoon. As the light outside was beginning to fade and Felicity was about to go home for the night, the bells on the shop door jingled and Jerry came into the shop.

She cheerily said "hello" to Heather
and Louisa, then headed straight for the
very books that Felicity was keeping an
eye on.

Raising her
book to eye level
and peeping over the
top, Felicity watched Jerry
as she took three books off the shelf
and stuffed them under her raincoat!
Felicity could not believe what she
had seen and hurriedly grabbed her
own coat as she fluttered out the shop
to follow Jerry. She found it very
difficult to keep the other fairy in

sight as she zoomed along a maze of cobbled roads and tiny alleys.

All of a sudden, Jerry turned a corner and went into a little house hiding amongst a row of shops, none of which Felicity had even known existed! She quickly hid behind a lamp-post as Jerry turned to close her door, and then ducked under the window overlooking the pavement.

"What a tiny house!" Felicity thought to herself. "And whatever is Jerry doing inside?"

Felicity slowly stretched up to the window and peeped inside. The curtain was closed but there was a tiny gap at the edge, just big enough for Felicity to see the mountains and mountains of books stacked up inside. Jerry was busy adding the new books to the piles and fluttering back and forth from a long table at the back of the room. Felicity couldn't quite see what she was doing – but she knew she had to find out.

She boldly knocked on the door and seconds later Jerry opened it a tiny crack, to see who was there.

"Hello!" Felicity said as cheerily as she could, while jumping up and down to try and see what Jerry had been doing with the old, tatty books.

"Can I help you?" Jerry asked, staring curiously at Felicity.

"Well, yes, I, erm," Felicity quickly tried to think of an excuse to go inside. "I'm desperately thirsty and I wondered if I could have a glass of water. I saw you come in here and recognized you from the bookshop."

"Hang on," Jerry said, shutting the door.

Seconds later she reappeared with a glass of water in her hand.

Felicity smiled, trying to hide her disappointment. She decided it was best just to be honest.

"I didn't exactly tell you the truth," she began. "I followed you here after I saw you take some books from the bookshop. You can't keep taking them, it's wrong!"

she blurted out all in one breath.

Jerry's wings quickly drooped as she let go of the door and stepped back to allow Felicity into the tiny room.

"I didn't mean to keep taking them! I just couldn't bear to see them in such bad condition and I had to do something about it. Only before I knew it I had so many books, and now I don't know where any of them came from. It's a disaster!" Jerry sobbed.

"So what exactly have you been doing with them?" Felicity asked, peering over to the table at the back where several books were lying open, clamped to the table.

"I'm mending them!" Jerry said, jumping up again. "I use traditional techniques to rebind them, individually stitching each page into place and gently restoring their covers. You can barely see the tears in this one any more!" she said proudly, holding a book out to Felicity.

Felicity looked at it in wonder. It was a very old book, but it looked just like new.

"Why didn't you just tell the bookshops and libraries what you were doing?" she asked.

"I took the first one as a surprise. I thought it would be nice just to borrow it and put it back completely mended before anyone even noticed it was gone," Jerry smiled. "But then it got a bit out of control. The library was closed one afternoon, so I went to the bookshop instead and then I couldn't remember which books I'd got from where," she sniffed.

"Don't worry," Felicity said reassuringly, putting an arm around Jerry's shoulder. "I'll help you return the books to their right homes."

✳ ✳ ✳

Felicity spent the next day contacting all the libraries and bookshops in the area and asking them to post her lists of all the books that had gone missing. Next she helped Jerry to mend the rest of the books she had taken.

Then Felicity and Jerry went through the books together, piling them up ready to take back to where they belonged. Felicity helped Jerry to write a letter to every bookshop and library, explaining what she had done and asking if they would like her to repair their damaged books. Before the day ended, Jerry had received replies from every place she had visited, saying they would love her to become their official book repairer.

"I can't thank you enough, Felicity," Jerry grinned, buzzing with excitement. "I never dreamt this would happen!"

* * *

The next morning, Felicity met Polly, Winnie, Daisy and Holly in Sparkles.

"Felicity, whatever have you been doing?" Polly asked as Felicity fluttered though the door, her wings flopping as she yawned. "You look like you haven't slept in weeks!"

"I was up all night finishing a book!" Felicity smiled.

As a thank you, Little Blossoming Bookshop had decided to give Felicity their first edition copy of *The Adventures of Shirley Helmes*, and Felicity hadn't been able to sleep without finishing it!

"That is, of course, after I

solved the case of the missing books!"
Felicity beamed.

Felicity's friends leant forwards, as
Felicity began to tell them about her
very own detective adventure!

Emma Thomson's

Felicity Wishes

Felicity Wishes and her friends

go on a holiday of a lifetime

to visit Felicity's new penfriend in

Enchanted Escape

Perfect Penfriend

Felicity Wishes had spent hours hunting for her special pink pen but she still couldn't find it anywhere.

"Borrow mine," said Polly in a hushed voice, as they were studying in the library.

"But it's not pink!" whispered Felicity.

"Does that matter?" asked Polly, frowning.

Miss Page, the library monitor, glared in their direction and put her finger to her lips. "Shhhhhhh!"

"Yes, it does matter," wrote Felicity on a scrap of paper and handed it to her friend.

"Why?" Polly scribbled back.

Felicity wiggled a beautiful sheet of sparkling pink paper in front of her friend's nose.

"I need to write a special letter," wrote Felicity, looking round to check that Miss Page wasn't watching them any more.

Polly suddenly stifled a squeal. Felicity's favourite pink pen was nestled neatly behind her ear! She tweaked it out and passed it to her friend, leaning over her shoulder to see who she was writing to.

Felicity was scribbling a response to an advert in *Fairy Girl* magazine. It read:

Penfriend Needed: Friendly fairy would like true friend to share dreams. My hobbies are knitting, cloud-trekking and singing whatever comes into my head.

Please reply to: Beatrice, The Cottage, Rainbow Wood, PM 12

Being the friendliest fairy in Little Blossoming, Felicity had found Beatrice's appeal hard to ignore. By the end of lunchtime she'd written a four-page response, telling Beatrice all about herself, her best friends, the School of Nine Wishes, and her favourite-flavoured ice cream.

"It's very good!" said Polly, after Felicity had shown the letter to her friends during break-time.

"Are you sure it's OK?" asked Felicity. "You don't think it's too over the top?"

"No, honestly!" assured Holly. "It's wonderful!"

"I would love to get a letter from you," said Daisy. "Your letters are so magical."

Felicity skipped happily to the nearest post box and made an extra-special wish just for Bea before posting her letter.

* * *

Every day Felicity watched for the Post Fairy before she left for the School of Nine Wishes, and it wasn't long before a large yellow envelope landed on her doormat in a cloud of glitter.

"Isn't it great!" said Felicity excitedly to her friends when she finally arrived at school. "Bea's written four whole pages, on both sides too!"

Felicity's friends gathered round her, flapping their wings with excitement, as Felicity read out loud her very first penfriend letter.

"Gosh, it's so exotic!" said Holly, admiring the beautiful paper. "They don't sell writing paper like this at the Fairy Stationer's in Little Blossoming!"

"And her handwriting is so lovely! Do you think she writes like that naturally or do you think all fairies where she lives write like that?" pondered Polly.

"And look at the delicate flower she's

attached to the letter. I've never seen anything as pretty as this ever. I wonder what it is?" asked Daisy.

Felicity picked up her fluffy pink pen straight away. "I'll write back to Bea and find out the answers to all your questions. I have a few questions myself – I want to know more about her friends, they sound so lovely!"

* * *

Over the next few weeks, Felicity and Bea exchanged letters almost every other day. Felicity couldn't believe they had so much in common!

Dear Beatrice

My best friend is Polly – she's good at everything and often has her head in books, studying to be a Tooth Fairy. Then there are my other two friends, Holly and Daisy. You'd love them. Holly is the queen of fashion in Little Blossoming and always looks stunning. Daisy is a real dreamer and loves spending time in her garden, chatting to her flowers. What are your friends like?

Write soon. Love Felicity x

A few days later, Beatrice's reply dropped on Felicity's doormat. She flew downstairs as fast as her wings would take her and opened her letter straight away.

Dear Felicity,

Oh my goodness! Your friends sound fabulous and just like my friends! My best friend is Amber and she won first prize for the best smile competition this year. My other friend, Star, dreams of setting up her own fashion label one day, and Jasmine is green-fingered and works part-time at the local garden centre. I can't believe how similar they are!

Write soon.

Lots of love, Bea x x

After reading Bea's letter, Felicity suddenly had an idea! "Wouldn't it be wonderful if I met Bea, Polly met Amber, Daisy met Jasmine and Holly met Star! she thought, smiling to herself. "I am sure we would all get on really well and half-term is coming up so we could visit them then."

Quickly Felicity grabbed her pen and immediately set about writing back to Bea to share her big idea with her…

＊ ＊ ＊

Holly, Polly and Daisy met for a milkshake at their favourite café, Sparkles. It seemed a bit too quiet without Felicity, who had been too busy writing to Bea to join them. The fairies had seen less and less of Felicity since she'd started writing to Bea. Whenever they did see her she was either poring over another letter from Bea or consumed with drafting her next letter. Holly and Daisy were beginning to feel a little left out.

Holly sighed and picked up a magazine and idly began to leaf through it.

"I've got it!" she said turning the magazine around to face the rest of her friends. "A holiday! Let's all go away together somewhere exciting where we can all have fun together just like we used to."

Daisy and Polly were delighted. It was a brilliant idea.

Read the rest of

Emma Thomson's

felicity Wishes

Enchanted Escape

to find out all about

the fairies' adventure.

If you enjoyed this book, why not try another of these fantastic story collections?

1. Designer Drama

2. Star Surprise

3. Clutter Clean-out

4. Newspaper Nerves

5. Enchanted Escape

6. Whispering Wishes

Friends Forever

Sensational Secrets

Happy Hobbies

Party Pickle

Wand Wishes

Dancing Dreams

13 Spooky Sleepover

14 Fashion Fiasco

15 Pink Paradise

16 Spectacular Skies

17 Dreamy Daisy

18 Perfect Polly

19 Winnie's Wonderland

20 Holly's Hideaway

21 Fairy Fun

22 Starlight Songs

23 Crowning Cure

24 Fairy Fame

Perfect Ponies

Storytelling Stars

Glittering Giveaways

Look out for these five special editions

Summer Sunshine

Holiday Hullabaloo

Christmas Calamity

Winter Wishes

Snowy Showdown

See Your Friendship Letter Here!

Write in and tell us all about your best friend, and you could see your letter published in one of the Felicity Wishes books.

Please send in your letter, including your name and age, with a stamped self-addressed envelope to:

Felicity Wishes Friendship Competition

Hodder Children's Books, 338 Euston Road, London NW1 3BH

Australian readers should write to...
Hachette Children's Books
Level 17/207 Kent Street, Sydney, NSW 2000, Australia

New Zealand readers should write to...
Hachette Children's Books
PO Box 100-749 North Shore Mail Centre, Auckland, New Zealand

Closing date is 31ˢᵗ December 2007

ALL ENTRIES MUST BE SIGNED BY A PARENT OR GUARDIAN.
TO BE ELIGIBLE ENTRANTS MUST BE UNDER 13 YEARS.

For full terms and conditions visit www.felicitywishes.net/terms

Friends of Felicity

Dear Felicity,

My best friend is called Green Nan. She is my Great Grandmother — and she really is Great!

She is fun, good at puzzles and good at games. She makes me laugh a lot and loves me lots.

In April 2007 Green Nan is 80 years old and I will be 8. I think that means there is zero difference between us!

Love from

Holly xx ♡ ♡

WOULD YOU LIKE TO BE A FRIEND OF FELICITY?

Felicity Wishes has her very own website,
filled with lots of sparkly fairy fun and information
about Felicity Wishes and all her fairy friends.

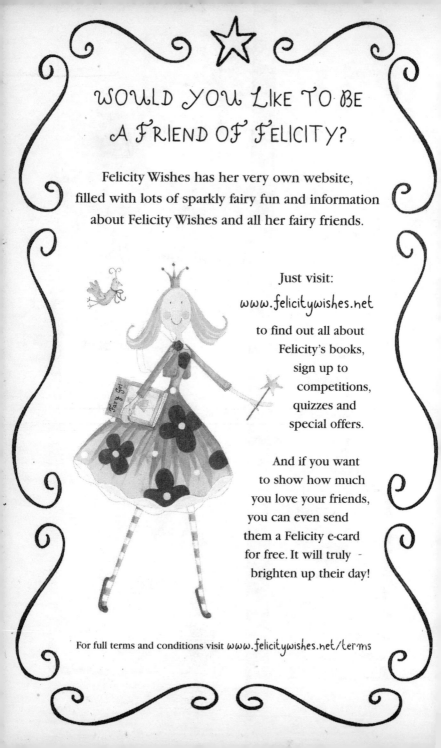

Just visit:
www.felicitywishes.net
to find out all about
Felicity's books,
sign up to
competitions,
quizzes and
special offers.

And if you want
to show how much
you love your friends,
you can even send
them a Felicity e-card
for free. It will truly
brighten up their day!

For full terms and conditions visit www.felicitywishes.net/terms